To Mark, Yuna and Adriel, who already know where to come when they're not invited to a birthday party.

Susanna Isern

To Lucia, for giving me so many birthday parties.

Adolfo Serra

I Wasn't Invited To the Birthday
Somos8 Series

© Text: Susanna Isern, 2014
© Illustration: Adolfo Serra, 2014
© Edition: NubeOcho, 2014
www.nubeocho.com – info@nubeocho.com

Original title: *No me han invitado al cumpleaños*
English translation: Robin Sinclair
Text editing: Caroline Dookie

Distributed in the United States by
Consortium Book Sales & Distribution

First edition: 2016
ISBN: 978-84-944446-4-7
Printed in China

VALUES
FUN &
DIVERSITY

I Wasn't Invited To the Birthday

Susanna Isern   Adolfo Serra

nubeOCHO

The children leaving the school are all very excited. There is a birthday party, but Mark isn't invited.

In the afternoon the park is empty. There isn't a single noise. Even the birds seem to have gone to the party.

"Hi! What a surprise! I thought that..." Mark says shyly.
"You see... I wasn't invited to the party either" explains Yuna.

Yuna and Mark are at the park. But they are not alone...
Suddenly Adrian appears and he is very excited.

"Hey guys! There's no time to lose. We need to climb to a
high place right now!"

The kids are a little confused, but they climb up a tree anyway. Once there, they sit on the thicker branches.

"So, now what?" Mark asks curiously.
"Something is going to happen" Adrian assures them.

Suddenly, they notice something unbelievable happen:
the sea has headed across the beach and is moving
very fast across the buildings of the city.

In a short while, the water has flooded everything. The park has become a giant aquarium, but the most amazing thing is that an enormous whale with a tiny hat has emerged from the water and has stopped in front of their tree.

"Do you have an invitation to go to the birthday party?"
It asks.
"No, we don't, we aren't invited… " says Mark a little sadly.
"So you can come aboard!" The whale says, inviting them to hop on its back.

The enormous whale with the tiny hat swims like a ship, with the three friends on its back, picking up other little boys and girls on its way.

All of those who were not invited to a birthday party.

Finally, after a long trip, they arrive at a beautiful small village on the top of a big mountain. It looks like a mysterious place, where no one seems to live.

It is so high that clouds come in and out through the windows of the houses.

The children run on the streets, through the fluffy clouds. Soon they discover that they are in a very special place and that they are not alone. The animals who live in the village are the weirdest they have ever seen!

Some wear shirts and trousers, others wear hats, and skirts. Some of them even wear high heels, glasses and even watches!

Adrian, Yuna and Mark are speechless! There is a party being celebrated in the square. The animals are very lively.

There is food, drinks, music and balloons.

"Is it a birthday party? Mark asks a nice crocodile with a funny face.
"No, the Ostrich´s birthday party is in the forest." it replies.
"And why aren't you going?" Yuna wants to know.
"Well, we aren't invited. You can't always go to all the parties. But this doesn't mean that we should be sad and we shouldn't enjoy ourselves" a tiger with a tie explains.

The kids enjoy an unforgettable afternoon in the village. Amidst all that fun, no one remembers the birthday party that they were not invited to.

When the sun begins to set, the whale whistles, announcing it's time to go back. The kids say goodbye to the animals.

On their way back home, everybody is happy. They can still touch the clouds and hear the happy music from the animals' village.

One by one, the whale leaves the children
in the same place it had picked them up.

"What an adventure!" Mark sighs.
"Yes, fantastic!! No one will believe us!" exclaims Yuna.
"It will be our secret" Adrian winks.

Adrian, Yuna and Mark climb down from the tree and go back home.

At nightfall, while the city is slowly going to sleep, they can hear the laughter of all those children who were not invited to a birthday party.

"Dear Little boys and girls
If you are not invited to a birthday party, don't be sad.
Just close your eyes and let your imagination fly.
When you least expect it, I'll pass to pick you up!

The whale with the hat".